Hugo O'Huge,
The Children's Giant

When Stephen and Rebecca found the
sleeping giant they fetched all the other
children to look. Were they scared? Not a
bit of it! They all shouted: 'WAKE UP,
MISTER GIANT!' into one enormous
ear, and up leapt Hugo O'Huge, the last
giant left in Britain, full of magical stories
and adventures. And for the children the
world would never be quite the same
again.

*Read Aloud books have large, easy-to-read type
and plenty of illustrations. They are ideal for
reading aloud or for young readers to attempt for
themselves.*

SHAUN TRAYNOR

Hugo O'Huge,
The Children's Giant

Illustrated by Linda Birch

Methuen Children's Books

931657
JS

First published in Great Britain 1984
by Methuen Children's Books Ltd
11 New Fetter Lane, London EC4P 4EE
Text copyright © 1984 Shaun Traynor
Illustrations copyright © 1984 Linda Birch
Reproduced, printed and bound in Great Britain by
Hazell Watson & Viney Limited,
Member of the BPCC Group,
Aylesbury, Bucks

British Library Cataloguing in Publication Data

Traynor, Shaun
  Hugo O'Huge, the children's giant. – (Read aloud
  books)
  I. Title
  823'.914[J]   PZ7

  ISBN 0–416–45440–2

Contents

1 Meet the Giant

When all the giants of Britain had leapt up into heaven there was one giant left. His name was Hugo O'Huge, because he was so big, so huge.

When all the other giants had leapt away, he had been living on his own and locked in dreams. No-one had told him what was going on.

When he awoke, all too late, he leapt high in the air to join the others but the magic didn't work and he fell back to earth with a BUMP! Again he tried but the Vital Moment had passed and again he landed back to earth with a BUMP!

The people all around said, 'What was that that shook the earth?'

It was only old Hugo landing BUMP!

Slowly he climbed a hill that had no name and when he got to the top he stretched himself up to his full height, his arms high in the air and his long shadow, as long as a bus ride, fell across the earth.

The people walking in and out of the high giant's shadow muttered to themselves, 'Is it night or is it day? It can't be dark already!'

From his tall hill Hugo looked into the world,

he looked to the North, he looked to the South,
he looked to the East, he looked to the West,

but there were no giants left. He rubbed his eyes and looked again but there was nothing to be seen (in the way of giants.)

He said, 'Where have all the great giants gone?' and 'Where have they all gone?'

The true wind replied, 'Who knows where the great giants have gone?'

Then Hugo asked the sea and the sea replied, 'I ain't telling where the great giants have gone. Old Hugo, you have missed your time.'

And when Hugo spoke his breath made church bells ring, and the wind of his voice made flags flutter.

The people said, 'What is making our church bells ring? Who is fluttering our

8

flags? Where is this strange breeze coming from?'

Then Hugo stretched up and let a great cry out of him and the sound was like a hundred trains rushing by. And the people said, 'What is that noise? What is that *noise*?' they asked.

But Hugo was tired of noise and misadventure. He lay down upon his hill and waited for time to pass.

That night the foxes in their forests barked, 'Look! Look! There is one giant left. It's Hugo O'Huge!'

But Hugo didn't hear, Hugo didn't listen. He lay down on his hill in sadness and tried to work out where he had gone wrong, why he had been left alone, but as always...

days passed
and weeks came

and he grew more and more lonely and his cries became weaker... but for the people the weather became better – no more earthquakes, no more flags fluttering on a still day, no more mysterious events. Soon, but not too soon, old Hugo fell fast asleep and began to dream.

And while he slept the grass grew and he

became covered in brambles and the foxes barked, 'There's old Hugo under the grass, no-one knows he's there.' And the stars twinkled, 'Hullo there Hugo,' but he didn't hear a thing, for the old fellow had fallen fast asleep, was deep in sleep.

And so it was in days of Long Ago: the grass grew and brambles covered, and berries shot red on the landscape and nothing much happened high on that hill until one day, until one day . . . a little boy called Stephen climbed the hill and found the giant.

It was after school, and Stephen, with nothing much else to do, walked across fields and then, climbing higher and higher through gorse and dandelion, patches of clover and sweet-smelling thyme, found the giant.

Stephen stared and stared. He stared and stared. There were the feet, in enormous boots, there was the coat and the big black curly beard. And there were the eyes, closed, each one as big as the biggest shell. Stephen ran home as quickly as he could. He almost forgot to breathe, he was so excited.

The next day after school he asked his sister Rebecca to go with him. They climbed the

hill and there was the giant! The children stared and stared. They stared and stared, and then they ran back home.

The next day they brought all the children from the town. All the children climbed the hill and found the giant. The children stared and stared. They stared and stared, but this time they didn't run back home. Instead they poked about a bit until they found his ear and then they all stood beside it and they all shouted in one big loud voice,

'WAKE UP, MISTER GIANT!'

'What is happening?' whispered the wind.
'Who is trying to wake the great giant up?'

'Wait and see,' whispered the sea. 'Some
children are trying to wake the great giant
up.'

'We'll all wait and see and tell the tale,'
said the wind, who was a terrible gossip. He
couldn't wait to cross the earth to tell the
story of old Hugo and the children.

'Listen,' said the sea.

'Listen,' said the travelling wind.

The children tried again. This time they shouted even louder,

'WAKE UP, MISTER GIANT!'

The giant stirred and floundered about a bit, but he did not wake up. In the forests the fox cubs stopped playing and, because it was a special event, they sat with the rabbits and along came the mole, rubbing his daylight eyes, and along came the worm; all the animals came to watch the children of the town try to wake up the great giant of Long Ago.

For the third time the children shouted, even louder, straight at Hugo's ear,

'WAKE UP, MISTER GIANT!'

The giant woke up laughing.

'Ha! Ha! Ha!' he said.

'Hee! Hee! Hee!'

Then he stood up, arms aloft, and cried,

'I'm Hugo O'Huge, I'm as tall as a tree.
There's no-one left bigger than me!'

14

But the children stood their ground. They shouted back,

'MISTER GIANT, WE'RE NOT SCARED OF YOU!'

'What was that I heard?' whispered the wailing wind. 'I can't believe my ears.'

'Such children!' chuckled the sea as it spilled amongst the shells.

The children shouted again,

'MISTER GIANT, WE'RE NOT SCARED OF YOU!'

Hugo O'Huge shook and roared with laughter.

'Ha! Ha! Ha!' he said.
'Hee! Hee! Hee!
What's all this?
Children not afraid of me?'

But already the children were clambering and climbing all over him, up his boots, on his trouser legs, swinging on his coat. Old Hugo sat down in case any of the children should fall off.

When they were settled he asked them,

'What do you want then, waking me up out of my sleep for years?'

'Tell us a story,' shouted the children.

'Take us on a journey,' shouted the children.

'A story? A journey?' said the old giant. 'Now let me see!'

And he scratched his head and three birds' nests fell out of his hair. He caught them and put them down safely, one in his pocket and the other two in a bush.

'A story?' said Hugo. 'What kind of story? What kind of story do children like Now-a-Days?'

'Your kind of story, Hugo,' said the children. 'A story from Long Ago.'

'From Long Ago?' said Hugo, pleased, because actually those were the only sort he knew. 'Oh yes,' he went on, 'I know stories from Long Ago. I know stories from when the world was just beginning. I can remember a time when there were two suns shining high up in the sky and there was no moon and no bedtime,' and so he began to speak and this is the first story that Hugo O'Huge told the children who sat and stared at him in delighted astonishment.

16

'Settle down,' whispered the wind, who put away his gusty toys to listen.

'Listen, listen,' whispered the sea, who lay quiet amongst his shells.

So the story began.

2 The Hill of Dreams

'Once upon a time,' Hugo said, 'and indeed it was a very long time ago, almost before the world began, there were two suns. They burned as bright as day up in the sky; it was never dark, there was no nightfall, just the two bright parts of the one long day.

In the first part of the day the people

would go about their business, to their places of work, to school; in the second half of the day they would go for short walks and have picnics and meet people from other villages and have games and competitions. This went on for a long and happy time.

Then one day the people noticed that the second sun was getting weaker; it wasn't shining as brightly as it should and the world got dark and cold. The people were afraid and they asked the giants what was the meaning of all this.

The giants said, 'Something has gone wrong on high. The second sun is sick and now will be called a moon, that is the way it is to be.'

'But what shall we do,' asked the people, 'in that second part of our long and happy day when it is dark and cold?'

The giants said, 'Meet with us in one year's time and we will give you our decision.'

In one year's time the people met with the giants and the giants said, *We will give you dreams.*

'Dreams?' said the people. 'But what are dreams? Do they stop you from being hungry? Do they keep you warm?'

'Dreams,' said the giants, 'are very easy to come by. All you have to do is lie down and shut your eyes.'

'Shut our eyes?' exclaimed the people in excitement, for they had never had to close their eyes before.

'Yes,' said a giant. 'You lie down and close your eyes.'

'Lie down?' said the people, for they had never had to lie down before.

'I can't close my eyes,' one person said.

'Nor can I,' said another.

'Look,' said the giant. 'All you have to do is lie down . . .' and the people lay down, 'and close down the little lids that separate day from night,' and the giants reached forward with fingers as light as butterflies' wings and closed down the lids of the people's eyes, so everyone began to dream.'

'And do you know,' said Hugo, 'they liked it so much it was a terribly hard job to get everyone to wake up again, to teach them the time of the morning, to get the children out in time for school.'

'I'm always late for school,' said a tall girl called Ruth.

20

'You're a sleepy-head,' said old Hugo, smiling. 'Still a Child of Dreams.'

'That was a lovely story,' said Rebecca.

'Yes it was,' said Stephen. 'Tell us another one.'

'Oh yes,' said the children. 'Do, do!'

'Ah no,' said the old giant. 'It's your turn now. You tell me a story.'

The children giggled and one girl called Kamala said, 'We don't know any stories, you tell us another one.'

'Oh do!' said the children. 'Please.'

The giant was soft-hearted but he believed in fair play.

He said, 'Fair play, children. It's your turn now. If you don't know any stories, tell me your dreams.'

'Our dreams?' said the children.

'Yes,' said Hugo. 'I christen this hill the Hill of Dreams. Here we will share our secrets, here everything will become beautiful or funny, here everything will have a happy ending, I promise you. Now tell me your dreams.'

And one by one the children stepped forward, as in a trance, and told the giant their dreams.

1st child	*I dreamt I was a fish at sea*
2nd child	*I dreamt I was a mule*
3rd child	*I dreamt the fairies danced with me*
4th child	*I dreamt I was at school.*
5th child	*I dreamt I ate a honey cake*
6th child	*I dreamt I ate ice-cream*
7th child	*I dreamt I ate five lollipops*
8th child	*I didn't have a dream.*
9th child	*I dreamt I was a pussy cat*
10th child	*I dreamt I was a dog*
11th child	*I dreamt I was a hairy ape*
12th child	*I dreamt I was a frog.*
13th child	*I dreamt I was the Queen of May*
14th child	*I dreamt I was her King*
15th child	*I dreamt I was a foreign spy*
16th child	*I dreamt that I could sing.*
17th child	*I dreamt I swam across the sea*
18th child	*I dreamt I climbed a hill*
19th child	*I dreamt I drank a cup of tea*
20th child	*I dreamt we won ten nil.*

Then one child said, 'I dreamt I was paint-
ing a picture of clouds and sky when suddenly
my brush became a wand and I entered an
enchanted world and could fly.'

'Why that's a poem!' said Hugo.

'Yes,' said the child. 'I didn't mean it to
rhyme. It just came out that way.'

Another child stepped forward. She said, 'I
dreamt I could swim.'

'And can't you?' asked Hugo.

'No,' said the child and then she giggled.
'Well, just a little bit, half a length with
bands.'

'With bands?' said Hugo amazed, for he
was thinking of bands that played music.
How could a band follow a child across a sea?

And 'Half a length? Amazing!' For he was
thinking of half a length of an ocean where
giants used to swim.

'Half the distance of a sea?' he asked again,
truly amazed.

'No, silly,' said the child. 'Half the length of
the baths – with *arm*-bands!'

Now the other children were rushing forward, dreams and secret wishes spilling from
their lips and their dreams became stories
and their story had become a poem. Dusk was

falling and the children had spoken their lines. We know now what they told the giant as the wind came closer and was hushed, as the sea was silent amongst his shells.

Now, because it was nearly bedtime, they said altogether:

We dreamed that dreams would never end
We dreamt that on this hill
We dreamed a dream and dreamed a dream
Until, until, until . . .

At the end of it all Hugo noticed that one girl was crying.

He brought her close to him and said, 'What is wrong, my child?'

'My name is Gemma,' said the child. 'And I didn't have a dream.'

'Well then,' said Hugo, 'you can have a wish instead.'

'Do you do wishes as well?' asked the children.

'No,' said Hugo, 'but far away in time and space there lives a beautiful witch called Ursula, who is called the Queen of Wishes. She can grant a wish and we can go there, you and I.'

'On a journey?' asked the children.

'Yes,' said Hugo. 'On a journey far past time. We can all go, except one. Who will guard the Hill of Dreams?'

A girl called Janie stepped forward and said, 'I'll guard the Hill of Dreams.'

'Are you any good at dreaming?' asked Hugo kindly.

'Yes,' said Janie. 'I like dreaming. I have lots of dreams.'

'Good,' said Hugo, and then he said, 'If that's the way of it, you may lie where I have lain and you will have a mighty dream.'

'Oh goody!' said Janie, and she lay where the great giant had lain, waiting for a dream.

No-one remembered that the next day was Janie's birthday; no-one knew what her dream might be. Hugo and the children took off on their incredible journey to meet Ursula, the Queen of Wishes. Janie stretched out amongst the brambles and the grass and the flowers; already she felt tingly as if magic was about to happen.

Gemma was excited too. All the children knew something was happening in time and space.

3 Ursula, the Beautiful Queen of Wishes

Whether or not Janie really saw the giant take off is hard to imagine, whether it was in the beginning of her dream or in reality that she saw him leap up into the sky, who can tell? But here is what really happened.

Hugo gathered up the children, well some of them climbed up. Some sat in his jacket pockets with their heads poking out so that they could see where they were going; others perched in his trouser pockets, and the pockets outside his trousers; some he carried in his arms; one child sat on his shoulder and held on to his hair and off they went. How did he go?

With one great leap he leapt to the north.

'Wheeee!' said the children as the wind rushed through their hair.

Then he jumped to the south.

'Wheeee!' said the children as the wind rushed through their hair.

Then he jumped to the east and then to the west.

Where was the child Gemma all this time? Tucked in his jacket pocket with her head poking out. She didn't miss a thing.

'Wheeee!' said the child Gemma as the giant went leaping far into time and space looking for Ursula, the wicked Queen of Wishes. Wicked? We shall see.

But the children were not alone. The wind picked up his joyful playthings and followed, knocking men's hats off and tossing slates from roofs – he sometimes did play dangerous games! The sea went out and in upon his tide to keep an eye on what was going on.

Back at the Hill of Dreams the animals – the rabbits, the fox cubs, a deer, a rat – came closer and looked at the child lying where the giant had lain; they watched her sleep and when the badger and the night owl and winter-calling hawk came too, all the animals and birds decided to forget old quarrels and to guard her until the great giant brought the children safely home. Hugo, by this time, was far away.

At last he found what he had been look-ing for: a quiet inlet by the sea-coast (where

there was country too) and there on the
beach sat Ursula, the Queen of Wishes, on
a wooden chair with the sea coming in all
around her, rushing round her skirts and
legs.

'Oh make me dry,' she said, and the sea
went out.

'Make me wet,' she said, and the sea came
in again and splashed around her.

'Make me wet, make me dry, wet, dry, hot,
cold,' and the sun shone brightly and then
nipped behind a cloud.

'Warm,' said the Queen of Wishes and

everything was back to normal again. She'd had her little game.

Then she dozed in her chair and then she woke again and said, 'Make me rich,' and jewels and precious brooches fell upon her clothes and golden coins from a different age sprinkled and clinked upon the hardening sand.

'Normal,' she said and everything was still.

Slowly Hugo tiptoed down and put the children near the Queen of Wishes. When she saw them she began to cry.

Then she wiped her eyes and said, 'I'm sorry, my little dears, it's just that I'm so happy to see you and who is this? Is this Hugo O'Huge come to the Land of Ages and bringing such gifts? Oh, dear little children, what would you like, let me use my powers to grant your wishes.'

The children rushed too quickly forward and the Queen of Wishes selected only a few lucky ones.

'Tell me your wishes,' she said.

The first child said, 'I want to be like you.' Immediately she grew old and then young again.

Hugo said, 'Once long ago Ursula was

31

beautiful, then she grew old and she wished so hard to be beautiful again that the giants granted her wish. Now she is neither young nor old, simply beautiful. But they considered her rather vain and wicked. They have commanded that she must live alone.'

A second child stepped forward. 'I want to be rich,' she said. Immediately (as before) coins from a different age and jewellery sparkled on the beach. The child made castles of them and curved in them and twisted in them and threw them up in the air and all around, and then as quickly as they came, they disappeared.

The child said, 'Where has my wish gone?'

The beautiful Ursula said, 'Wishes are easily made, difficult to grant; they do not last, there are so many more coming behind.'

The third child stepped forward. 'I want a wand to change everyone into frogs.'

'Will you change them back again?' asked Ursula.

'If I have two wishes,' said the child.

'Each child can have one wish,' said Ursula. 'Who will help?'

The tall girl called Ruth stepped forward.

'I'll help,' she said and stood back from the froggy wish.

A wand appeared in the third child's hand and she waved it and said, 'Frogs.'

Immediately all the other children (except Ruth) became frogs and leapt about the beach croaking and bumping into each other.

'How high they jump!' said Hugo in delighted amazement.

At the end of the wish Ruth took the wand and said 'Normal!'

Ursula chuckled, 'My, you do learn quickly,' and everything went back to the beginning again.

A fourth child stepped forward. 'I want a wish to end all wishes,' she said.

'What do you mean?' asked Ursula, looking at her as if she were her own child.

The girl said, 'I wish I had all the wishes and that wishes for me would never end.'

'Very clever!' said the children.

'I can't grant that wish,' said Ursula, 'because if you have all the wishes people are left without their dreams.' No-one wanted that.

The next child stepped forward.

'This is the last wish,' said Ursula, who was easily tired.

'I wish,' said the child, 'that everyone who has a wish will see that wish come true.'

Then Ursula said, 'I cannot grant that wish either. What I can say is that everyone in the world is entitled to one wish in their lifetime. Think well, children, before you make that Vital Wish.'

Hugo stepped forward and knelt down.

'I have a child here,' he said, 'who cannot dream. Can she have a special wish?'

'Yes,' said Ursula, whose tiredness vanished when she met people in need. 'What is your name, child?'

'My name is Gemma,' said the girl, 'and I'm very sensible. I would like for just one day to be like someone else.'

'All right,' said Ursula, the Queen of Wishes, who was wicked in a delightful way. 'For one day you can be a princess and marry a prince, and your coach will be made of cloud and sun and your roadway will be through the pale afternoon stars. Child, it is your wedding day.'

Immediately all the children became characters from stories and there was Hugo, a giant amongst them dressed in fantastic clothes. Gemma looked and couldn't believe her eyes. Then the sun went down and a couple of clouds, assisted by the wind, formed themselves into a coach.

Gemma, dressed now in a long wedding dress and with the tiara of a princess on her hair, stepped into the clouds and took off on her sky-honeymoon. Where was her prince? Perhaps waiting over the rainbow. We shall never know for when she returned all was still and everyone was back to his normal self again.

One girl rushed forward.

'Oh, Ursula, Queen of Wishes, please grant me one more wish,' she pleaded.

'What is that?' asked Ursula.

'I want long hair,' said the child.

Instantly (because Ursula was kind) the child had lovely long golden hair which wrapped itself all around her so that she looked, amongst the shells and the sunlight, just like a mermaid. And then she was normal again.

'That didn't last long,' she said.

'Told you so. Wishes don't last long!' said Ursula, the Queen of Wishes.

Hugo gathered up the children again to take them home. They said goodbye to the now sad Queen of Wishes and left her in her chair, which had become a rocking-chair, and she, herself, had grown suddenly old; they left her with the sea rushing in around her and then slowly going out again.

'Goodbye, Ursula,' called the children and Hugo leapt up into the sky.

'Goodbye, Ursula and thank you,' said Gemma looking back once.

'Oh yes,' said the children, not forgetting their manners, 'thank you, Ursula,' and they left her all alone.

4 The Little Girl Whose Birthday Didn't Come

Back at the Hill of Dreams Janie was still sleeping. Now that the magic time had passed, all the animals had returned to their homes. Hugo landed gently and the children ran over to waken Janie.

When she awoke she stretched and sat up and rubbed her eyes and didn't know where she was for a minute. Then she saw the giant and the children and remembered that she had been left to guard the Hill of Dreams. Quickly she looked all around, yes it was still there, well she was sitting on it, wasn't she? It is strange for a person just waking up to see a giant; but all the children were getting used to Hugo now, they believed in him.

What everyone wanted to know now was if Janie had had a mighty dream. So they all sat round waiting to hear her tell her story and Hugo sat round them all like a wall.

'I dreamt,' said Janie, 'that my birthday hadn't come. I dreamt that I awoke and quite simply, it wasn't there.'

'You dreamt that you awoke,' said Ruth, 'but if you *dreamt* that you awoke then you were still dreaming.'

'I know,' said Janie, 'but when I did awake I was in my bedroom and there were no presents, no-one saying, Happy Birthday, no tingling feeling of being eight!'

The children giggled, they knew exactly what she meant.

And so began the story of the strangest day in Janie's life.

First she called downstairs to Mum.

'Mum!' she called. 'Mum, Mum! Come here! My birthday hasn't come!'

Mum came upstairs with her apron on. 'What's this, Janie, no birthday? Oh my! What a disappointment!' And then she asked, 'Have you looked for it under the bed?'

'Don't be silly, Mummy,' said Janie. 'Birthdays don't begin under the bed.'

'Have you looked on top of the wardrobe?'

'Don't be silly, Mum,' said Janie. 'Birthdays don't begin on top of wardrobes, that would be even sillier. Birthdays come through the window like the sun and make you feel happy and there are presents all around.'

When Mum had gone back downstairs again, Janie went to the window and looked out at the sky. 'Oh,' she whispered,

'Giant of the Clouds and Giant of the Sky,
Look round the world and tell me why
my birthday hasn't come.'

And the Giant of the Sky came and stood in Janie's garden and his face was against her bedroom window and he was old and fluffy and spoke in a funny way because clouds and tiny puffs of wind were all around his mouth and hair. He said,

'I oh-blow-blow don't know why-aie-aie your birthday hasn't commmmme.'

What he meant to say was simply,

'I don't know why your birthday hasn't come.'

But because of the wind that came rushing round his teeth and the clouds that came drifting into his mouth, it came out silly like,

'I oh-blow-blow don't know why-aie-aie your birthday hasn't commmmme.'

So Janie looked out of the window again, past

the fluffy face of the Giant of the Sky and said,

'Giant of Earth under the sky
Please tell me why
my birthday hasn't come.'

The Giant of Earth lived in Yorkshire. He came with mud on his boots and stood in the garden beside the Giant of the Sky. His face was up beside Janie's window.

He said, 'I don't know why your birthday hasn't come, lass,' and then he sang a little song:

'I've had a look round
but it's not to be found
I've looked in muck
and I've looked in grass
and I've looked where people
have made their brass
but your birthday I cannot find.'

Then he went on, 'Lass, if your birthday ain't on land and if it don't be in the sky, why not think about summat (which is Yorkshire for "something") out at sea?'

So Janie called out of her window again,

'Giant of the Waves, Giant of the Sea
Come to my garden and try to tell me
why my birthday hasn't come.'

And the Giant of the Sea came to Janie's
garden and he was a very queer fellow indeed.
He arrived with frogman's flipper feet and a
snorkel. As he walked up the path his flipper
feet went splish, splosh and splosh, splish,
and when he took his snorkel off he spoke
funnily too. He said,

**'I don't-ish know-ish why your birthday
hasn't come-ish.'**

41

When he spoke it was like the sound of water running away down the sink, a gurgling noise, for he still had lots of water in his mouth and seaweed and shellfish and tiny yellow fish and blue fish swum and hung and clung to the frogman's suit. What he wanted to say was simply,

'I don't know why your birthday hasn't come,'

but it came out strangely, like

'I don't-ish know-ish why your birthday-ish hasn't come-ish.'

It was awful. Now the Giant of the Sea and the Giant of Earth and the Giant of the Sky stood round talking – they hadn't seen each other for a long time – and of course people began to gather at the garden gate.

Janie's mother came out and said, 'What's going on here, you big people? What's happening beneath the morning stars?'

The giants were very polite.

'How-ow-ow-ow do you do?' said the Giant of the Sky.

'Ow-do,' said the Giant of Earth.

'**How do you do-ish?**' said the Giant of the Sea.

'Oh!' said Janie's mum. 'I'm very well thank you, ta very much. Would you like a cup of tea?'

'**Thank you-you-you,**' said the Giant of the Sky.

'**Yes thanks,**' said the Giant of Earth.

'**Thank you-ish,**' said the Giant of the Sea.

So Janie's mum went inside and made tea and brought tea and biscuits out to the garden and after that everyone began to worry about Janie again.

The Giant of Earth said to her, '**What about under the ground?**'

'Under the ground?' said Janie, surprised.

'**Under-der-der-der the ground,**' said the Giant of the Sky.

And the Giant of the Sea, not to be left out of things, said, '**Under the ground-ish.**'

So Janie went down to the cellars of her house and called to the Giant of Under-the-Ground,

'Giant of tunnels, Giant of caves,
Giant of darkness, Giant of graves,
Please tell me why my birthday hasn't come.'

43

And the Giant of Under-the-Ground appeared, not out in the garden where there was daylight but there in the cellar with Janie. And he was a kindly person but very very tired. And he seemed to be surrounded by roots of trees and branches and they twined and inter-twined round his long brown coat. And tiny white flowers grew round his long beard and round his fingers there were twigs.

'I have no birthdays under the ground,' said the strange thin giant. 'The little creatures who live with me have their birthdays on the moist grass and in hay-fields. Roots of trees don't have birthdays, their birthdays are measured above the ground. I live among skeletons, and skeletons only have death-days. Would you like a death-day, child?'

'Oh no,' said Janie, 'I'm much too young for that,' and much to her relief the Giant of Under-the-Ground disappeared and the room became warm again.

Janie climbed the stairs to thank the other giants for trying to help her and then, as in a dream, she only remembered lying where Hugo had lain, and she seemed to remember

Hugo leaping high into the sky and she seemed to hear voices saying goodbye; she was sure she heard the Giant of the Sea go splish-splosh, splosh-splish back to an ocean, she thought she saw the Giant of the Sky disappear as in a cloud and she thought she heard the Giant of Earth say he was getting a bus back to Yorkshire.

She did hear them saying goodbye.

'Goodbye, lass.'

'Goodbye Janie-ish.'

'Goodbye-bye-bye-bye oh-blow-blow.'

And everything was still.

'When I awoke,' said Janie, 'I was here on the Hill of Dreams, and Hugo was landing and all my friends were around me.'

Suddenly from behind Hugo, Janie's mum and dad appeared. They climbed over Hugo as over a wall. They were the first adults ever to climb to the Hill of Dreams. And they had brought some of their friends as well, other parents. All the adults carried presents in their arms and one child's father who drove an ice-cream van had brought up lots and lots of ice-cream.

'Happy birthday,' said Janie's mum and

all the children and all the parents began to
sing:

'Happy Birthday to you,
Happy Birthday to you,
Happy Birthday dear Janie
Happy Birthday to you.'

and then

'Janie guarded the Hill of Dreams
where nothing is as it seems.
Janie waited all night long
to hear the children sing this song.

'Happy Birthday to you,
Happy Birthday to you,
Happy Birthday dear Janie
Happy Birthday to you!'

Everyone was happy. When the birthday party was over and it was time to go home, Ruth said, 'Is this the end?' She was really sad. 'Can we come and see you again, Hugo?'

'You can always come back here,' said Hugo, 'for this is the Hill of Dreams.'

5 The Bubble That Stole a House

The next day was a Saturday. Stephen and Rebecca woke up in their semi-detached house. Even in their own familiar bedroom they still felt a strange tingling, a distance from reality, as if they were half asleep and half awake, both at the same time, as if they were half in dreams, half in the real world.

On Saturdays Stephen's mum worked in a supermarket and she took Stephen and Rebecca round to Gran's house for the day. There they would wait until Mummy came home at half past five. Gran lived in a detached house in a crescent and she had a garden.

They came in magically and she gave them biscuits and orange squash and then a treat, a cup of tea. For a long and happy time Rebecca and Stephen and Gran sat around munching and sipping. Gran always seemed to have an endless supply of biscuits and drinks.

At the end of the meal Gran cleared the things away and left the children picking up crumbs from the carpeted floor. Then they joined her in the kitchen where she was doing the washing up. This is where the second half of our story begins. Gran did a very peculiar thing. Well, she was a very peculiar person, neat and nifty and full of life and willing to take chances. What she did on this magical Saturday, no child had ever seen before.

When all the dishes were washed and wiped and put away, Granny went back to the washing-up bowl and dipped her hands in the soapsey-sudsey water. Then she took them out and with her hands still dripping with soapsuds, she put her two thumbs together and cupped her hands and began to blow. As she blew, she opened one hand like the wing of a bird and out came the most gorgeous little bubble.

The bubble floated and drifted across the room. Stephen and Rebecca watched it. They watched it float to the other side of the room and then it hit the wall and went POP!

The children shrieked with delight. Now they wanted to try too.

Stephen dipped his hands into the soapsey-sudsey water, put his two thumbs together, cupped his hands and began to blow. He blew and he blew. Then he opened one hand like the wing of a bird or like the door of a bird's cage being opened, and out came A BUBBLE!

It floated and drifted across the room and then it hit the wall on the other side and went POP! The children laughed and jumped up and down in excitement. Now it was Rebecca's turn!

Rebecca dipped her hands in the soapsey-sudsey water in the washing-up bowl and took them out dripping with suds. She put her two little thumbs together and cupped her hands and took a really deep breath, breathed in really deeply, and then she began to blow; carefully at first, then with increasing strength.

Then she opened one hand like the wing of a bird or like the door of a bird's cage being opened and out came the most gorgeous, the biggest bubble anyone had ever seen.

Granny and the children watched the huge bubble float and drift across the room until it got to the other side and hit the wall. But this

time it didn't go POP! Instead it got bigger
and bigger!

It got bigger and bigger until it was as big
as the room and then it got bigger still and the
room was inside it. Then it got bigger still and
the hall and the front room were inside it. Still
it got bigger until the upstairs and the whole
house was inside the bubble, neatly encased.
Then it took off!

The bubble took off and inside the bubble
was the house and inside the house were
Stephen and Rebecca and, of course, Gran.
Gran was at the window looking out. She

waved to the four neighbours who had noticed the strange goings-on. She said, 'Goodbye Earth!' Rebecca and Stephen sat in chairs and wondered what would happen next. Another adventure had begun.

What happened at half past five? The children's mum came round the corner of the street with her shopping bag and all the worries of a Saturday and up to number 47 – no number 47!

'Where has Gran's house gone?' gasped Stephen and Rebecca's mum, who was called Joyce. It had gone far up into the pale afternoon stars.

Joyce stared and stared. She stared and stared. What on earth could she do? She did what any sensible person would do in such a predicament, she called a policeman.

She called, 'HELP! POLICE! COME QUICKLY! A BIG BUBBLE HAS STOLEN GRAN'S HOUSE. And inside the bubble is the house, and inside the house are Gran and Stephen and Rebecca, and they're drifting out past the moon and on toward the stars, oh BOO HOO HOO!'

Round the corner walked Police Constable

Bliggs, PC 1081. PC Bliggs had had an easy day, nothing much had happened and it was nearly home time and he wasn't expecting anything very out of the ordinary to happen now. He certainly didn't expect to get involved in the strange case of the bubble which stole a house.

So he walked round the corner minding his own business, (well really I suppose he should have been minding everybody else's) and suddenly he spotted Joyce jumping up and down and shouting, 'HELP! HELP! POLICE! POLICE!' This was something he could readily understand.

'Yes now, madam,' said PC Bliggs. 'What seems to be the trouble?'

'A big bubble has stolen my mum's house, number 47, and my little children are inside it.'

'That seems very unlikely,' said PC Bliggs.

'Well, if you don't believe me,' said Joyce, 'just look up there!'

The police constable looked up and saw the bubble. Inside the bubble he saw the house and inside the house he saw Gran and Stephen and Rebecca. They were at the window. But this time they weren't waving. In

fact they were looking rather apprehensive. PC Bliggs was so surprised his helmet fell off!

'Well! Well! Well!' he said (which is something policemen and all adults say when they can't think of anything else). 'Well! Well! Well!' In fact he meant that things *weren't* well; in fact, if you think about it, things were very *un*well indeed.

'What are you going to do?' said Joyce worriedly.

'Do?' said PC Bliggs. 'I'm going to radio for a detective.'

'Oh good,' said Joyce.

'Oh good,' said Ruth who had also come round the corner.

'Oh good,' said the other children who had come to watch the fun.

'What's a detective?' asked Janie, who was very good at guarding hills and having dreams but didn't know many big words.

'A detective?' said PC Bliggs. 'He's a very clever kind of policeman who looks for clues and solves crimes. He's good at working out problems.'

'We could do with one here,' said Ruth.

PC Bliggs used his radio transmitter to speak to a detective in the police station and within five minutes a police car had arrived with a detective inside. He got out and asked what all the trouble was about and why they needed someone brainy like him. When he heard the news he was flabbergasted. When he saw the bubble up amongst the late afternoon stars he was astounded. When he saw the house inside the bubble and when he saw Stephen and Rebecca and Gran, he said, 'This is incredible!' Then he began to think!

'I have solved the problem,' said the detective and everyone listened very carefully to what he was about to say. 'What we need,' he said, 'is a Bubble-Catcher!'

'A Bubble-Catcher?' said the people. 'Brilliant!'

'Brilliant!' said PC Bliggs.

'Brilliant!' said Joyce.

'But what's a bubble-catcher?' asked Ruth, who had been thinking hard as well.

'A bubble-catcher is a very special kind of person,' said the detective. 'Now what kind of person do you *think* would be a bubble-catcher; a very small person or a very tall person?'

'A very tall person!' said most of the children who were there.

'Brilliant!' said the detective. 'Now what sort of person would be a *very* tall person indeed?'

'A giant!' said Ruth.

'Brilliant!' said the children, delighted.

'Yes!' said the detective.

'Brilliant!' said Joyce, and then she said what any sensible person would have expected her to say, 'Brilliant, but ... there aren't any giants around here any more.'

'Oh dear,' said the detective.

'Oh dear,' said PC Bliggs.

'That's been the story of my life,' said the detective. 'I get a really brilliant idea and then, at the very last minute, it just doesn't work out.'

'Oh dear,' said Joyce.

None of the adults had noticed that Ruth had begun laughing. None of the adults noticed that the children had all begun to laugh and skip around happily.

Then the children all shouted together, 'There is a giant! There is a giant! We know a giant and he's the dearest, sweetest, old giant who ever lived. And he lives on the Hill of Dreams!'

'Hill of Dreams?' said PC Bliggs suspiciously. 'I don't know any Hill of Dreams.'

'Giant?' said Joyce. 'Don't be silly, children. This is a serious matter.'

'Giant?' said the detective. 'Oh if only what you believed were true,' and he sighed wistfully.

'But sir,' said Ruth, 'there is a giant. And there *is* a Hill of Dreams. We've been there, all of us, and we've met him and talked to him and he's very tall. He's tall as a tree and he can jump.'

'Bliggs!' said the detective. 'Get your notebook out. Take down the details. A jumping giant. Just the ticket, eh?'

PC Bliggs took his notebook out and his pencil and asked Ruth, 'What's the name of the giant, Miss?'

'His name is Hugo O'Huge,' said Ruth.

'And what is his address?' asked the police constable.

'The Hill of Dreams,' said Ruth truthfully.

'And where is that?' asked the policeman.

'It's not far from here,' said Ruth. 'If you can organise cars we'll go there and show you.'

'Cars?' said the detective. 'That's no problem,' and he got his radio transmitter out and ordered four cars for everyone there: destination – the Hill of Dreams!

'Wow-eee!' said the children.

'Wheeee!' said Gemma, and off they went.

6 The Bubble-Catcher

Four police cars arrived and all the children and all the adults piled in. The Lord Mayor also came because he would not want to miss an occasion like this. He came in his huge Lord Mayor's car with a flag flying. A journalist from the local paper came as well. He came in a van with his cameras in the back.

Nothing could go wrong now. The eyes of the world were on the children, the police, Stephen and Rebecca's mum and the Lord Mayor as they all sped out of Gran's street and on into the country, off toward the Hill of Dreams.

Of course no-one had a map with the Hill of Dreams marked on it; the name had only been invented a few days before, but the children knew the way. When the cars got some way out of town and into hilly country they had to stop and everyone had to get out and begin to walk.

Higher and higher they climbed, through gorse and chalk-pits and flowers and bramble until they came to where Hugo was lying. He was asleep and, as ever, he was covered in branches and brambles; they helped to keep him warm.

The adults watched in amazement as the children scampered over the giant looking for his ear. Then they all shouted:

'WAKE UP, MISTER GIANT!'

And the old giant woke up smiling.

'Hullo, kids,' he said.

'Hugo,' said Ruth, 'we need your help. Look up there. Do you see that big bubble?'

Hugo looked up. He lay on one elbow and the whole hill seemed to move. He looked up and saw the bubble and inside the bubble he saw the house and inside the house he saw Gran and the children, huddled together, a bit afraid.

'Do you think you could jump up and save them, Hugo?' Joyce asked.

'I expect I could,' said Hugo.

'Well then, will you do it?' asked the detective.

'Who is this?' asked Hugo suspiciously.

61

'Oh, don't worry,' said Ruth. 'There are just some police here and a reporter and, um, a Lord Mayor. It's been quite a day in town.'

'Hmmm,' said Hugo, thinking. 'If it's all so public, maybe I should charge a fee.'

'What does that mean?' asked the children.

'What he means,' said the Lord Mayor pompously, 'is that he will require payment for his services.'

'And who are you?' asked Hugo, picking the Lord Mayor up between his finger and thumb.

'I'm the Lord Mayor,' said the Lord

Mayor, terrified, for he was high off the ground. 'You can have anything you want, Mister Giant, honestly.'

Hugo put the Mayor down and thought for a moment. Then he said, 'Well, it's a long time since I had anything to eat, several hundred years in fact. Perhaps while I'm jumping, some of you could organise a breakfast, or a lunch or a tea.'

'Yes, yes,' said the Lord Mayor. 'Anything you say, Mr O'Huge.' And so the deal was made.

The children watched as the giant stood up. Again a shadow fell over the land. The adults were terrified but the children were used to it now.

Hugo began to hop.

HOP! HOP! HOP!

and the whole world seemed to shake on its axis. Then he began to run. From one field to another, he ran.

THUMP! THUMP! THUMP!

The farmers in the fields took off their caps and scratched their heads in amazement. Tractors stopped and pig-men spilled their

63

pails. There was no doubt about it now; there was a giant still on earth. On Hugo went until he had enough momentum to take off. And up he went, his shirt-tail and his waistcoat, like a beautiful cloak, flowing out behind him.

The wind now began his part in the story. He was a great eavesdropper as well as a gossip, but like most people, in his heart of hearts, he wished to be kind. Now he hurried away north and surrounded the bubble with gusts and brought it to where Hugo was leaping and floating.

Hugo caught the bubble and then, floating on his back, he used the bubble itself as a kind of parachute. Some people heard him whisper, 'Thanks wind,' and slowly Hugo and the bubble floated earthwards.

The wind helped again. It guided Hugo and the bubble to the street where Gran lived. Inside the bubble, Stephen and Rebecca and Gran were standing at the window, standing very still in case they upset the great giant's balance, but they were smiling. They knew their troubles, and their adventures, would soon be over.

Hugo positioned the bubble perfectly and the house fitted in beautifully between number 45 and number 49. Everyone on the Hill of Dreams watched breathlessly as things worked out. Now they drove at speed to Gran's street and the Lord Mayor stepped out of his car with an enormous needle and pierced the bubble. The bubble went

POP! It went POP!

Quite the loudest pop anyone had ever heard and tiny bits of soapsuds splattered into their eyes which made everyone blink and rub. When they opened their eyes again the bubble had disappeared into thin air and through the front door of the house stepped Gran and Stephen and Rebecca.

What a reunion! Everyone was happy and talking and laughing. No-one noticed that Hugo had gone back alone to the Hill of Dreams.

It was the next day before everyone remembered the Lord Mayor's promise.

'Sunday lunch for Hugo!' Ruth shouted.

'A giant's banquet!' shouted Stephen and Rebecca.

And the Lord Mayor, true to his word (not like the wicked Mayor in 'The Pied Piper of

Hamlin') began to organise Hugo's meal. A committee was formed to work out a menu. This is what they wrote:

The Giant's Banquet
Menu

1 lake of soup
25 bread rolls
25 pats of butter

—❀—❀—

100 sausages
50 lamb chops
500 bags of chips
10 fried eggs

—❀—❀—

A milk lorry full of milk & a straw

—❀—❀—

Extra large Roly-Poly pudding
and a small lake of custard

All the ice-cream in a shop

—❀—❀—

A barn full of biscuits

A reservoir of lemonade

How did they get the food to the Hill of Dreams? The parent who owned the ice-cream van brought it as far up the hill as he could, then the children brought the ice-cream up, wafer by wafer, cone by cone.

All the cafés and bakeries in the town opened up for this one Sunday to make the giant his meal and the army lent helicopters to carry the food. A huge hosepipe was to be his straw for the milk and for the lemonade.

An enormous tarpaulin was draped across the Hill of Dreams to act as a tablecloth and

Hugo ate off a ceremonial pewter plate. Everyone watched. It was fantastic.

At the end of it all his crumbs fed all the birds of the air.

Was this the end then of the children's adventure with Hugo O'Huge? This is the sad part of the story now.

So many adults, as well as children, now knew about Hugo that the Hill of Dreams was no longer a secret and magical place. People began coming up on Sundays for picnics and pointing at the giant and making remarks about him. Hugo became more and more alarmed.

One Sunday people came and there was no giant there. The next Sunday was the same, no Hugo! The following Saturday Stephen and Rebecca, hand in hand, climbed the Hill of Dreams and looked everywhere. There was no doubt about it, Hugo had disappeared. They looked everywhere but Hugo was not to be found. A great sadness filled the children's hearts. What could they do?

The children found it difficult to sleep at night. They were worried about Hugo. Was he far away? Was he as far away as the ends of the earth and the beginnings of space and

69

time? Had he found another hill or leapt away for ever on to the Cliff of Time? In bed the children dreamed and remembered their dreams. Janie remembered all the children singing,

'Happy birthday to you,
Happy birthday to you,
Happy birthday dear Janie
Happy birthday to you.'

She remembered the great Giants of Earth and the Sea and the Sky and the strange thin creature from under the ground. She remembered how she had lain and guarded the Hill of Dreams.

Stephen and Rebecca remembered the very first day they had climbed the Hill and found the giant. All the children remembered their first big shout,

'WAKE UP, MISTER GIANT!'

and then

'WE'RE NOT SCARED OF YOU!'

and they remembered Hugo standing up tall and they remembered him laughing.

70

'I'm Hugo O'Huge, I'm as tall as a tree
There's no-one left, bigger than me.'

Now there was no-one left different from everyday people, and life returned to normal.

Gemma remembered Ursula, the Queen of Wishes, and her strange enchanted flighting.

'Oh!' said Gemma. 'I wish we could see Hugo again!'

'Oh!' wished all the children. 'Please come back, Hugo. We miss you so!'

The wind and the sea were well aware of the children's dreams and wishes and they carried them to the very ends of the earth. Surely Hugo would hear?

7 Goodbye Hugo

Days passed and then weeks. The children became very anxious and lonely. They wondered what had gone wrong. They wondered if the adults had had anything to do with Hugo's disappearance. After all Hugo had always been *their* giant; they had found him, woken him up, listened to his stories, told him their dreams.

They began to wonder if Hugo didn't like grown-ups. They remembered how suspicious he had been of the Lord Mayor and he had never charged any of them for their dreams.

They wondered if perhaps his feelings had been hurt when the ice-cream man first saw him and had said, 'I can't believe my eyes.' Or had he been put off by the Sunday picnickers, who would say things like, 'This is rum, eh? A giant! Must be out of a circus!'

Hugo wasn't from a circus, he was from the

Cliff of Time, a giant in Time and Space. The children understood this and they also understood that Hugo had liked them, had enjoyed their company. When the television was on, or in maths lessons, even at times like that, the children, in the backs of their minds, still kept trying to work things out.

Their teachers and their parents were very patient. They also understood the thing about grown-ups; but Miss Prime, their teacher, had another idea. She said that perhaps a Vital Moment had come to Hugo from Time and Space, perhaps something had happened in the universe that made it possible for him to leap away and join his friends. Perhaps there had come a time when giants could leap above the world and he had had to go; he would not have had time to say goodbye.

'He could still write or something,' said Ruth.

'I'm sure he's trying,' said Rebecca.

The children listened to all the explanations but the truth was, *their* feelings were hurt. Seven weeks passed and nothing at all and then, in the eighth week of their Hugo-less-ness, a miracle! Or if not a miracle, a

73

sensational, impossible-to-explain Event. A message came from Hugo, a message from the outer limits of Time and Space. Here is how it happened:

Red class were doing maths. It was a Tuesday, any old Tuesday, when suddenly there was a fierce scraping on the roof. A few minutes later, through the window of their classroom, the children saw the caretaker run along the corridor. The children knew something pretty fantastic was going on because they had never seen Mr Banes the caretaker break into a run before. But there he was, speeding towards the playground!

Because it was an Extraordinary Event Miss Prime allowed the children to spill out into the playground so that they could see what was going on. In the playground the teachers were rubbing their eyes, they couldn't believe what they were seeing and no wonder! Two huge eagles had landed on the school roof but they weren't ordinary eagles; they were made of stone, yet could fly.

They were noble gargoyles which Hugo had sent from out of Time and Space. They were the guardians of Heaven and they had

brought a letter. It was the biggest letter the children had ever seen.

The caretaker climbed a ladder on to the roof and brought it down. The eagles flew away after first circling the playground.

'Take me with you,' Gemma called.

But the eagles were made of stone and so were stone-hearted; they simply obeyed orders and flew off. Besides, whilst they were away, the gates of Paradise were open. The children opened up the letter. It was dirty, damp and crumpled, and this is what it said:

Hello Children,

I am safe and well but far, far away. I can see you when you are in the playground and I have sent two eagles made of stone to deliver the letter. How are you?

Do write! Leave your letter on the roof and my eagles will collect it.

I think about Earth quite a lot and although I am not lonely amongst the other giants I do miss you. Thank you for the meal - it was lovely.

Do write Ruth and Gemma, Dreaming Janie, Stephen and Rebecca - by the way, thanks for finding me.

Keep in touch now I'm far away.

-Love -

Hugo O'Huge
(Giant)

The mystery was now revealed. Hugo had found himself within a Vital Moment and had taken off. Perhaps he had wished and wished. It was certainly the children's wishing that had told him to send this letter and as it had been such a long time in coming, he must be very far away.

'Millions and millions and millions of miles,' said Kamala.

The children went back to the classroom and maths was forgotten as the children penned their reply. Four bits of sugar paper were stuck together and a huge (for Hugo O'Huge) letter was written. It would take many pages of this book to show you the whole letter, but it looked something like this:

Dear Hugo, This is Stephen, Hullo!

Dear Hugo, This is Rebecca, Hullo from me too!

Dear Hugo,
This is Ruth. I
I am another
Stephen, Hullo   dont like division. Dear
Hugo, how many nines
I am Peter   in twenty-seven?

I am Yasmin   Dear Hugo, This is Gemma
Thank you for making my
Oh I cannot look at the sky
out I remember her. Love
I am Debbie   Dear Hugo, Gemma
This is Junie. Your hill is still
I am Kamala   safe. Glad you enjoyed the
ice cream. Love Junie

HULLO!   Hullo!   Hullo!

Then the caretaker climbed the ladder again and put the children's letter beneath some stones for Hugo's eagles to collect. That night, when the children were asleep, it was not eagles which Hugo sent but two ravens, the colour of the night and again made from stone. They circled the empty, eerie playground, found the letter and took it back to Hugo.

Seven more weeks passed but there were no more letters.

The children wished, 'Oh dear Hugo, why can't you come back, if only for one day?' Then they wrote a special letter:

Dear Hugo,
        Please come back
if just for one day
P. L. E. A. S.E .
    Love from
All the children

        x x O O

A few days later Hugo sent a note, it said:

Dear Kids,
  I will try to come back in a Vital Moment.
  For the meantime I will send a postcard. Look out for it.
  Love —
          Your friend Hugo
            the Giant

On Thursday lunch time the playground became bathed in beautiful colours as if from a hundred prisms of the sun, and from out of a blue sky came a picture postcard from Paradise. It landed in the playground and unfurled like a magic carpet. The headmaster in his study kept taking off his glasses and rubbing them with his hanky and then putting them back on again.

He kept muttering to himself, 'What is going on here? What is going on?'

The children raced to look at the card. It was very large and a rectangle and on it was the children's first glimpse of Paradise.

There were castles there and Turkish mosques and curling towers up to the sky and on the ground were golden water-melons being cut by knives and there clouds floating everywhere high and low so that you could bite them. They looked as if they were made from a kind of candy floss.

And there were giants lying about the place, some of whom the children recognised. There was the giant from Jack-in-the-

Beanstalk, there were the seven dwarfs from the story of Snow White and millions of tiny fairies dancing in webs of gold. On one street there was a statue to Ursula, the Queen of Wishes, who must have been there once and loved by them all.

There were so many things to look at that, when the bell went for afternoon lessons, the headmaster and the caretaker didn't really mind the children staying out longer. Indeed by this time the headmaster was feeling rather pleased that the children from his school had found the giant. He could see himself presenting the postcard to the local history museum where it would last for ever.

Before the end of school the children shouted up to the sun, 'Thank you, Hugo!'

And then they shouted, 'Please come back. If only for one day!'

Then it was back to lessons before the last bell sounded.

8 Hugo's Return

Nothing happened. Weeks passed. The children were really fed up. Miss Prime tried to make life more interesting by using different coloured chalks when she was explaining division. Then she had the brilliant idea of lunch-time picnics and it was at one of these country picnics that the next part of our story begins.

One day at lunchtime Miss Prime, who was an expert in mathematics, took the children to follow lay-lines to the Hill of Dreams. Lay-lines are ancient ways of maps. After lunch Miss Prime had her really brilliant idea.

She said, 'You know something, children. We've never looked for Hugo on the Other Side of the Hill.'

It was true! In all their adventures the children had climbed up the town-side of the Hill and then climbed down that same side again.

Now immediately after Miss Prime had had her brilliant idea the children, like a starry stream splashing and bobbing over stones, ran and jumped and clambered down the Other Side of the Hill of Dreams. There they entered a forest, cool and woody, with somewhere in the distance the sound of a river and a waterfall. Through the tangled paths of shrubs and twisting roots the children picked their way carefully, looking for signs of a giant.

Suddenly Stephen shouted excitedly, 'Look! Look! I've found something!' And indeed he had, he had found a giant boot!

'What is it?' asked Gemma.

'It's a boot,' said Ruth. 'Can't you see that?'

'Oh yes,' said Gemma. 'A giant boot.'

Well, it wasn't easy really to work out exactly what it was at first. It was an extremely large boot. You could have parked a bus in the foot part of it, that is if you had a bus to park, and the ankle and leg part was so tall and wide you felt that you could plant a Christmas tree there, year after year.

'It's Hugo's boot!' cried Kamala, and all

85

the children rushed further into the deepening wood.

Kamala found the other boot.

'Look! Look!' she called. 'Hugo's left boot!'

And, looking up, the children saw through the tree tops a clearing of splintered branches as if someone had crashed down from the sky. Then they followed a path of brushed-aside trees and broken, churned-up twigs and leaves and cool, cool moss.

And then they came to a proper clearing by a river and there was the waterfall falling and cascading down from a magic mountain in rivulets and patterns of silver and wetness. And there was Hugo sitting by the bank with his feet under the waterfall giving them a good wash, and in his hands were his socks – he had been giving them a good scrub as well.

When he heard the children he looked round his shoulder and his face broke into a huge Hugo O'Huge smile and he said,

'Hi, kids!'

And the children stood for a moment looking at him, the way you look at someone you love but haven't seen for a long time, then they shouted, 'Hugo! Hugo! Hugo!'

And then they were clambering all over him and giving him kisses. All the way to the river's bank Rebecca had been threading daisies into a chain, now she climbed up to his neck and hung the chain around his right ear.

'Thanks, Becky,' said Hugo the Giant.

'This, by the way, is Miss Prime,' said Ruth, 'although,' and here she whispered, 'we sometimes call her Ms Prim.'

'How do you do, Mr O'Huge,' said Miss Prime. 'I'm very pleased to meet you. I have heard lots about you. I've even seen your picture in the paper.'

'Thank you, my dear,' said Hugo. 'Now how about a school visit?'

'Oh yes! Yes! Yes!' shouted the children.

'I'll have to ring the headmaster and ask his permission,' said Miss Prime.

'*Wring* him?' said Hugo. 'What do you mean, *wring* him? Do you mean, twist his neck?'

'Oh no,' said Miss Prime quite breath-lessly. 'I don't mean *wring*, I mean *ring*. It's a modern word about telephones.'

'Ah,' said Hugo. 'Then you need a tele-phone box. On my way down from the skies above I noticed one at the corner of Elm Tree

Avenue. Allow me.' And so saying he picked Miss Prime up between his finger and his thumb and easily lifted her to the nearest 'phone box.

There she made her call. The headmaster was really pleased.

'Yes,' he said. 'Yes, yes, please do come. Now.'

Then, like a chair-lift, Hugo carried her back to the forest glade where the children were basking in make-believe.

'We have to hurry,' said Miss Prime. 'First lessons are starting.'

'I can't go without my socks,' said Hugo, as he looked at them now dripping on a thorn hedge.

'That's easy,' said Ruth. 'Remember Ursula?' And she drew herself up to her full height and conducting the other children as if they were in an orchestra, she said, 'Dry!' And the children breathed a magic wish and the socks were dry.

'Thank you, Ursula,' whispered Kamala as soon as everyone was ready. The children were beginning to realise that when you deal with things that pass human understanding, anything is possible.

When they arrived back at school, which
was just a skip and a jump away (for a giant),
the headmaster and the caretaker had spread
a red carpet out on the playground, which is a
way of saying WELCOME. It was the first
time the headmaster had done any of this
kind of work and he was rather out of breath
but he was smiling.

'Welcome, Mr O'Huge,' he said.

Hugo let the children down and they ran
and made a circle in the playground. All the
other children shouted:

'Three cheers for Hugo O'Huge, our
favourite giant!' and:

'HIP! HIP!
HOORAY!
THANKS FOR COMING BACK!'

'How did you get here?' asked Ruth. 'What happened in a Vital Moment?'

'I have learned the secret,' said Hugo, 'of how to move between the Earth and into that world called Make-Believe. You quite simply *make* yourself *believe*. You mutter words, you turn around, then a skip and a jump. I'll show you. But it means I must return again. Away from you. It means I must say goodbye again.'

The second bell rang.

'That's second lessons, Mr O'Huge,' said the headmaster. 'And look, the Press are arriving.'

Sure enough, Bob the journalist was turning into the playground in his van.

'He'll want to take a picture of you, Hugo,' said Kamala.

'Well that's very nice,' said Hugo, who liked the idea of leaving a little something behind.

The children didn't want Hugo to go but they knew they had their own lives to lead and they would have photographs. They did want to see how he took off; yet they were anxious lest they should not see him again. Perhaps now he had learned the secret he could leap up and down between Earth and Paradise any time he wanted.

'When you go,' asked Ruth, 'will you come back again?'

'Yes, I will,' said Hugo and the children were happy.

'Can we come with you?' asked Rebecca.

'No,' said Hugo, 'that wouldn't be fair. There are too many people here, like your parents and your teachers, who would miss you too much. Time is different on the hills of Paradise, days don't count. It's hard to judge Time: a day could be a year, or a week the whole of someone's life. I promise you I will come back before you have grown up. Now that might be tomorrow or it might be in three years' time. So take your time growing up.'

'Will you tell us a story, Mr O'Huge?' asked Bob the journalist.

'Ah no,' said Hugo. 'We've had enough of them. It's time I was off. You can watch me disappear if you like.'

The children and their teachers sat transfixed. A third bell went – the end of

lessons altogether. Parents had also arrived at
school, they stood by their prams.

Hugo moved gracefully from playground
to field and then to the Hill of Dreams.

'Goodbye, Hugo,' cried the children.

'Goodbye, Mr O'Huge,' said the teachers.

'Cor, look!' said the parents with their
prams.

On top of the Hill of Dreams Hugo spun
round and leapt. When he was about five
hundred heights high, something strange
happened. Gravity lost its hold on him and
other forces took over. He seemed to soar and
glide like a magic kite getting higher and
higher. So he was carried away.

On the playground the children spread out
the postcard he had sent them, like a map of
where he was going. They looked at it until
home time. Then they went home and

days passed
and weeks came

and nothing much happened on the Hill of
Dreams or in the town which is a part of it.
Would the children ever see Hugo again? Yes,
of course they would! Even in their dreams.

And as for the Hill of Dreams it is now quite

simply an earth barrow once again, old and disused. Yet children sometimes climb there and memories grow wild there as well as flowers; and the stars take note and the wind passes by and the thoughtful sea is often silent amongst its water and its shells.